In the Rest Room at Rosenblooms

by

Ludmilla Bollow

SAMUEL FRENCH

FOUNDED 1830

NEW YORK HOLLYWOOD LONDON TORONTO

SAMUELFRENCH.COM

ISBN 978-0-573-66332-1   Printed in U.S.A.   #25642

IMPORTANT BILLING AND CREDIT REQUIREMENTS

All producers of *IN THE REST ROOM AT ROSENBLOOMS must* give credit to the Author of the Play in all programs distributed in connection with performances of the Play, and in all instances in which the title of the Play appears for the purposes of advertising, publicizing or otherwise exploiting the Play and/or a production. The name of the Author *must* appear on a separate line on which no other name appears, immediately following the title and *must* appear in size of type not less than fifty percent of the size of the title type.

The Premiere Performance

of

In The Rest Room At
R O S E N B L O O M ' S

An Original Script
by
Ludmilla Bollow

Directed by Douglas M. Young*
Student Director—Jacqui Singleton
Set Design by Patton Lockwood*
Costume Design by Petie Grigg

CAST

Myra . . . . Jenny Glover-Droney
Violet . . . . Karla Myers
Winifred . . . . *Donna Brooks
Olga . . . . Reeny Manley
Patrons of ROSENBLOOM'S . . . . Melanie Bailey
Clare Baxter
Ellen Reed

"Old Lace and Lilacs"
written and sung by Jacqui Singleton

ACT I

Time: May 1, 1970—Afternoon
Place: The lounge of ROSENBLOOM'S Department Store

ACT II

A half hour later

ACT III

A few minutes later

PRESENTED BY
THE LONGWOOD PLAYERS AND
THE DEPARTMENT OF DRAMATIC ARTS

FEBRUARY 25-28 JARMAN AUDITORIUM
1976 8P.M.

CAST

MYRAH – A bit loud. Slightly raunchy. In her 60's, and fighting every bit of advancing age.

VIOLET – A cultured lady with a regal carriage that is a bit difficult to maintain. Late 70's.

WINIFRED – A thin timorous woman, with the airy quality of a sunbeam. Early 60's.

CLARE – Heavy set. Reddish hair in non-fuss style. Thick-lensed glasses. Authoritive and officious. Mid 60's.

PATRONS – Nine non-speaking roles. (Can be played by the same person, with quick changes or each can also be played separately.)

TV VOICE – Offstage only.

SYNOPSIS OF SCENES

TIME: Monday, May 1st
PLACE: A rest room lounge in an old downtown department store.

ACT ONE
SCENE 1: Late Morning
SCENE 2: Half Hour Later

ACT TWO
SCENE 1: Few Minutes Later

ACT I

Scene One

(**SETTING:** *The rest room lounge in an old downtown department store. There's a faded elegance, a comfortable feeling of home.*)

(*Once, way back, the whole room was redecorated. Most of the same decor remains, as if stopped in time. Still, it's a cheerful room, with painted wicker furniture, old-fashioned floor lamps– a mannequin or two. Huge potted plants and assorted smaller plants.*)

(*The hall entrance, with closeable doors, is STAGE RIGHT. An alcove entrance to the washroom area is STAGE LEFT. Window on back wall has pillowed bench beneath. CENTER is oval coffee table with three chairs around. Other furnishings include: desk and chair, small settee/lounge, arm chair, candy machine with mirror, coffee machine, and drinking fountain.*)

(**AT RISE:** *Department store SOUNDS are heard in background – cash registers, voices, music. These SOUNDS will be heard briefly before each entrance, as if a door opens and closes.*)

(**PATRON # 1** *walks through carrying bright flowery shopping bag with "ROSENBLOOMS" printed in large letters, goes to washroom.*)

(**MYRAH** *enters, stands in doorway, resting on her cane, surveying the empty room. She wears a ratty fur jacket, cheap silky print dress, and lots of flashy jewelry. Her black frayed slip shows. Her stockings have runs, and her high-heeled shoes are turned over at the edges. A floppy spring-like hat covers yellowed blonde hair and* *tangled remains of a drooping hair set. Heavy makeup masks once-pretty features. She carries a bulging shopping bag.)*

(She enters as though making a stage appearance, and the show is about to begin.)

*(**MYRAH** takes off her hat and places it atop a mannequin's head. She drapes her jacket and cane over the side of an arm chair, goes to the candy machine, and checks makeup in mirror. She settles in chair near the coffee table and takes out bag of grapes, putting them in dish on the table. She begins eating grapes, watching entrance.)*

*(**PATRON # 1** exits from washroom and stops for a drink at the drinking fountain.)*

MYRAH. *(loudly)* Listen honey, I wouldn't drink too much of that water, if I was you. Filled with lead. This store's got lead in all its pipes. Unhealthy! Poisons the liver.... Why, I've even written letters to Mr. Rosenbloom himself. But, store don't seem to care if their regular customers get lead poisoning or not.

*(**PATRON # 1** gives **MYRAH** a quizzical glance and walks out.)*

Trouble today. Nobody cares. Nobody.

(continues eating grapes)

(SOUNDS)

(brightens) Violet! I thought that was you, girl!

*(**VIOLET**, a leftover from the days of elegance, enters carrying several homemade bags of worn brocade, an umbrella, and an old suitcase-like box. She wears a dated purple velvet coat with a sprig of violets pinned to the lapel, lacy lavender blouse, purple skirt, and light colored sandals. Lavender gloves, a lavender purse, and amethyst jewelry complete the ensemble.)*

VIOLET. Good morning, Myrah. My, you're looking well today.

MYRAH. Yeah, well how I look sure ain't how I feel. Shoulda seen me, hobbling down the streets this morning.

VIOLET. Lovely day, isn't it.

*(***VIOLET*** *takes off gloves and coat, carefully drapes them over back of chair SL)*

MYRAH. Ol' Doc Brummer told me I gotta use a cane now.

VIOLET. For goodness sakes. Canes are for old ladies.

*(***VIOLET*** *straightens the room during the following business.)*

MYRAH. S'what I told him. Came in handy though. You know those cross lights what blink, "WALK," when they really mean, "Run like Hell!" Anyway, I'm only half-ways across the street, when this bozo, in his big black Lincoln, turns right smack in front of me. Know what I did? Whacked my cane right across his shiny rear end. *(laughing at remembrance)* Didn't know what the hell hit him.

VIOLET. Those cross lights certainly are not timed for anyone with arthritis, are they.

(takes bouquet of lilacs and smaller jar from bag)

MYRAH. Say that again. Worse this morning. Hands crippled up so, couldn't even get my girdle on. So– left the damn thing off. Aagh, never did like those tight rubber girdles– squeezin you in one place, while it all bulges out in another.

VIOLET. Right.

MYRAH. *(lifts dress, showing red lacy pettipants)* So, wriggled into these fancy French panties instead.

VIOLET. How– nice.

(embarrassed, goes to washroom with jar for water.)

MYRAH. *(calling after)* Present, from an old boyfriend of mine– when I was in burlesque yet. *(reading from embroidery)* Sem-per Fi-de-lis. Means "Always Faithful."*(boisterous laugh)* Hah! Not him! Not old Elevator Pants Charlie!

VIOLET. *(sets lilacs in jar on coffee table)* Lilacs were just beginning to peek out this morning. Mama's bush. Planted the year she and daddy were married….

MYRAH. Need more than flowers to perfume up this place. *(takes aerosol can from bag and sprays about)*

VIOLET. *(coughs daintily)* That's a mite stronger than your usual spray.

MYRAH. *(reads)* "Breath of Death." Free sample they left in front of next door. Germ killer mixed with perfume. *(Opens washroom door, sprays inside, shouting.)* Come on, you dirty germs– Drop dead!

(SOUNDS)

*(***PATRON # 2***, a weatherbeaten old lady, enters. She has mismatched, oversized shoes, ankle socks, a ragged long black coat, scraggly hair, and is clutching a grungy shopping bag.)*

MYRAH. Good lord, here comes Minnie the Moocher.

*(**MINNIE** walks into washroom without looking at them.)*

VIOLET. Poor soul.

MYRAH. She sure knows Monday's Josie's day off.

VIOLET. Josie has been getting more fussy lately. Nervous too. Well, all those rumors about Rosenblooms being bought by that foreign firm, and–

MYRAH. Stop worrying 'bout such things. 'Nough other stuff to worry about these days.

VIOLET. Isn't that the truth.

MYRAH. Yeah. Nother old lady got mugged last night. On her way home from church yet. Had her on TV News– crying her eyes out.

VIOLET. What is this world coming to.

MYRAH. You keep yourself home nights. That neighborhood specially.

VIOLET. Oh, I do.

MYRAH. Listen, she talks to you, don't answer, even if you don't think it's not polite. Else we get her here all morning.

VIOLET. Poor soul, I often wonder where she sleeps.

MYRAH. Criminy, this is a high classed store. Public library's for dead beats like her.

*(**MINNIE** leaves.)*

MYRAH. *(cont., sotto voice)* See that bulge. Toilet paper *and* paper towels today. Phew, really need fresh air in here now. *(**MYRAH** goes to window, struggles to open it)*

VIOLET. Josie's sign– "Do Not Open This Window!"

MYRAH. Yeah, well Josie ain't here today and I need fresh air. Dry heat in here's bad for the skin. Causes wrinkles.

*(window finally opens, **MYRAH** takes deep breath)*

VIOLET. I don't believe I will be staying very long today. But, maybe I can finish just one flower on one napkin. *(sets out embroidery things on coffee table)*

MYRAH. Hey Violet, what you got in that big fancy box?

VIOLET. Box? *(evasive)* Oh– just Melissa.

MYRAH. Who the hell's Melissa? And why you got her in a box?

VIOLET. She's– she's just– a doll. My grandmother's doll.

MYRAH. Sooo, let's have a look at her.

VIOLET. All the way from Paris she came.

*(**VIOLET** opens the suitcase-like box and takes out a beautiful French doll, dressed in lavender.)*

Here we are, Melissa. In Rosenblooms' Rest Room. I've told her all about this place.

MYRAH. Boy, she really is a beauty.

VIOLET. Say, "Mama."

(tips doll over, doll sing-songs, "Mama")

She cries too.

(doll cries)

But, we're not going to cry today, are we.

MYRAH. Violet– you ain't selling that doll, are you?

VIOLET. Sell– Melissa?

MYRAH. Yeah. You been selling everything else. Furniture. Paintings.

VIOLET. Well no, we were just going to visit– with Anton, the Antique Man.

MYRAH. So, now you're down to selling family too.

VIOLET. I really don't want to, but–

MYRAH. Then don't! You don't wanta do something, don't do it!

VIOLET. Well, you see, my property taxes– And, they've sent me several letters about my electricity bill. Some, not very nice.

MYRAH. I keep telling you– Sell that big old gingerbread house of yours.

VIOLET. Oh no! Not the Parkinson family home!

MYRAH. Well, you're gonna have to sell one of these days. When all your antiques are gone. Railroad stocks down to nothing.

VIOLET. (*ignoring* **MYRAH,** *sweetly to* **MELISSA**) Come, Melissa. (**VIOLET** *carefully wraps doll and puts back in suitcase.*)

MYRAH. What are you gonna do then? Starve? Go on welfare?

(*SOUNDS*)

(**PATRON # 3** *shuffles in tiredly, walks toward coffee table chair.* **MYRAH** *interrupts her as she's about to sit down.*)

MYRAH. Sorry honey, this seat's saved. That green chair, next to the plant, nobody sits there.

VIOLET. But, it's a very comfortable chair.

(**PATRON # 3** *leaves in a huff.*)

MYRAH. Wish Winifred would show up. Saving that spot for her day after day ain't that easy. (*takes out supermarket tabloid paper*)

VIOLET. It's been almost a week now. (*begins her embroidery*)

MYRAH. (*reading cover headline.*) "My Doctor Raped Me On My Wedding Night!" Hmmm, read that one right now.

VIOLET. I worry about her– Living all alone like that.

MYRAH. "It was my wedding night…. My doctor climbed into bed with me, and then– "

VIOLET. No one to take care of her. Not even a telephone.

MYRAH. Hmm– what?

VIOLET. Winifred – I can't help worrying about her. She's such a delicate person.

MYRAH. Oh, Winifred.

(SOUND)

(points) Hey, look at that, will you.

(PATRON # 4, *in mod outfit, short skirt, boots, sunglasses, walks through to the washroom.)*

VIOLET. They certainly dress peculiar these days.

MYRAH. No bra either. Next social security check, I'm gonna get me a pair of those boots. In white, no maybe red.

(WINIFRED *enters in a breathless flutter, carrying an old-fashioned gold birdcage and other assorted items. She wears a billowing summery dress in faded yellow voile, giving her the appearance of a fluttery butterfly. A flowing gold cape resembles huge bird wings when her arms are raised. A bright yellow ribbon holds back her gold/gray hair, styled in an uneven page-boy hairdo.)*

(She's a delicate creature, with the airy quality of a sunbeam. Her movements are between floating and dancing, her voice, soft and gentle. Sometimes, when her mind and thoughts are elsewhere, she seems to be soaring off into her own realm of space.)

MYRAH. Well, my god, it's Winifred!

VIOLET. Winifred dear, how are you?

WINIFRED. *(raises her arms in benevolent greetings)* Oh my precious friends, I've missed you so.

MYRAH. Where you been, girl? Geez, you still look white around the gills.

(WINIFRED *sets her things down with a flourish, removes her cape dramatically, and pirouettes so everyone can notice her billowing dress.)*

WINIFRED. Gracious, I had so many things to take care of– bring along– My head's still whirling– whirling– *(begins* *to sit)* Excuse me, I better touch up my hair a bit. And take some more of my asthma medicine.

(**WINIFRED** *exits to the washroom.*)

VIOLET. Poor child. She still looks pale.

MYRAH. Cause she never wears enough makeup. When you're feeling punk, that's when you gotta paint an extra smile on those drooping lips.

VIOLET. So terribly thin. I don't think she eats enough.

MYRAH. Know what I think her trouble is?

VIOLET. Her asthma?

MYRAH. No. It's those damn plants– and vines– and ferns– crowding up her teensy place.

VIOLET. Why, how could they –

MYRAH. Take up all her oxygen, girl.

(**PATRON # 4** *in mod outfit leaves. This time attention to her is only fleeting.*)

Then, besides, she's got all those dipsy birds flying around. Screeching. Molting. Dropping their dirt all over. Unhealthy.

VIOLET. I suppose.

MYRAH. Told you bout that time I took her home on the bus. Day she almost passed out down here.

VIOLET. Yes. Acted so very strange.

MYRAH. That place, honest to god, like something out of a Tarzan movie. Regular jungle! See, her Henry, he stuck seeds in each one of his letters– from those islands, during that Pacific war.

VIOLET. Yes, you told me.

MYRAH. So, she keeps planting those seeds. And they just keep growing. Why, some of those vines go right up into her attic. Well, what do you expect after all these years.

VIOLET. I think it's lovely– her still waiting for Henry.

MYRAH. Aagh, he's never coming back.

VIOLET. Winifred certainly believes he will.

MYRAH. Damn right. She's got this one corner fixed up

like a shrine. Honest to god. Henry's picture in his air force uniform. All his letters. *(pause)* And the tele-gram– "Missing in Action."

VIOLET. And never any word since.

MYRAH. Aagh, she should give up this foolish waiting. Find somebody else, while she's still young enough.

VIOLET. Sometimes, you don't want anybody else.

MYRAH. Hell, look at me, I've had three husbands, and I'm still looking for another. *(laughs boisterously)* And by god, one of these days, while these legs are still work-ing, I'm gonna find me one.

VIOLET. *(joining in on the joke)* Well, you're certainly not going to find one here, Myrah. *(laughs with a gentle titter)*

MYRAH. Aww, this here's only my stopping off place. Night time, that's when I go out looking for partners. I don' know, I just hate being alone at night. Always have.

*(**WINIFRED** comes out of washroom whistling a bright little tune.)*

VIOLET. Well, where are we going today, all dressed up?

WINIFRED. Why, to the zoo, of course.

VIOLET. Zoo?

WINIFRED. May first. My wedding anniversary. I always go to the zoo.

MYRAH. Lots better places to celebrate an anniversary.

WINIFRED. Oh, no. Henry and I met at the zoo. In the aviary. I was watching the peacocks. Henry was watching the flamingos. Then, we began watching each other.

MYRAH. Suppose you can meet a man anywhere. Never thought about the zoo. Gotta go there sometime.

WINIFRED. *(takes cover off bird cage)* These are my wedding presents. From Henry. So I wouldn't be too terribly lonesome, while he was so far, far away.

(holds up cage, birds begin chirping)

VIOLET. Such cheerful little birdies.

WINIFRED. They are company, but, I still get lonesome.

MYRAH. Course. Birds in a cage ain't nothing like a man in the bed, I'll tell you.

VIOLET. What are their names, dear?

WINIFRED. Romeo– and Juliet.

MYRAH. Figures.

(**WINIFRED** *coos with birds.* **PATRON # 5** *walks in during following to get cup of coffee from the coffee machine. She looks about, to sit down. After taking in scene, she decides to take coffee with her and exits.*)

WINIFRED. They'll quiet down. Just singing out their "How do you do's." *(sings.)*
"Let's all sing like the birdies sing, tweet, tweet, tweet– tweet tweet."

MYRAH. You better sit quiet, Winifred. You still look kinda peaked.

WINIFRED. *(Sits in saved chair.)* Ninny Winny. I almost forgot I've been ill. Then, I had to get up extra early– press my wedding dress– *(Stands and pirouettes.)*

VIOLET. Is that your wedding dress?

WINIFRED. Henry picked this out for me. From Rosenblooms. Canary yellow.

(looking away, fading into memories)

VIOLET. I would have worn a long flowing gown of white lace–

WINIFRED. He only had a two week furlough. Everything went so fast. The wedding– the honeymoon– Then, he was gone….

MYRAH. Satin. I wore pink satin first time around. Sixteen, I was. Sweat pouring off me by the gallons.

WINIFRED. The only thing left– this dress– my canaries– Henry's letters. And, the telegram. *(stops, looks off into space)*

MYRAH. *(claps hands in tune to rhyme)*
"Gone is gone– Past is past.
Future's only thing that'll last."

WINIFRED. *(begins spreading mail on coffee table)* Heavens, mail just piled up inside my front door. *(whistles softly as she opens letters)*

MYRAH. Got any "occupant" coupons you don't want, just flip them over this way. Sweepstake contests too. I enter every one of them– three times.

VIOLET. Three?

MYRAH. Sure. Under each of my married names.

VIOLET. But, what if you'd ever win?

MYRAH. Nah. I never win nothing. Cept free dance lessons one time. Then, with the damn arthritis, could only go sit and watch. That's no fun.

WINIFRED. *(begins breathing excitedly, hand to chest)* Oh, my gracious! Today! She's coming for me today!

VIOLET. Who's coming?

WINIFRED. My sister! Clare!

MYRAH. Calm down girl, or you're gonna have another one of your asthma attacks.

WINIFRED. She writes, she's taking me on vacation early this year.

MYRAH. Yeah– Where does she take you?

WINIFRED. To her place. "Clare's Canine Campus." She runs a dog obedience school.

MYRAH. And that's where you go for vacation?

WINIFRED. When mama died, Clare promised her she'd take care of me. But my birds couldn't live with her frightening dogs. So, to keep her promise, somewhat, every summer, she takes me to her place, for two horrible weeks.

VIOLET. We used to vacation– at our lovely lake home.

WINIFRED. But, I don't think she's planning a vacation this time.

MYRAH. Why not?

WINIFRED. Because– she told mama, when mama was still living with me, "Pack up your bags, we're going on a nice little vacation." *(stops)*

MYRAH. Yeah, where'd they go?

WINIFRED. To a home! Clare put mama away in a home. And she never ever came back.

VIOLET. Her own mother!

MYRAH. So, why would she do that to you?

WINIFRED. Because– she keeps telling me something's wrong with me, and I shouldn't be living alone anymore.

MYRAH. Hell, you don't want to go on no vacation– You don't have to!

WINIFRED. She wants me to sell my house too, move in with her– and her dogs.

MYRAH. Tell her to buzz off and leave you alone.

WINIFRED. Ever since we were children, Clare's always been able to make me do whatever she wants, even when I don't want to. She's even better at it now, since the dog school. She can take the wildest dog, and in a few weeks, has the animal cowering.

MYRAH. Well, you're no dog. And you can go and do whatever you want.

WINIFRED. She'll come here, when she finds I'm not at home.

VIOLET. To Rosenblooms?

WINIFRED. Yes. I write her about coming to the rest room every morning. Visiting. Watering Henry's plants.

MYRAH. No sweat, Winifred. Clare comes here, just tell her you don't care to go with her.

WINIFRED. It won't work. All she has to do is look at me and say, "Winifred!" and I do what she wants.

MYRAH. So, don't even let her see you. Hide some place. We can check out anybody what comes down that long hall.

WINIFRED. Hide? Where?

VIOLET. Behind the drapes?

MYRAH. Nah, that's no good. Let's see. Hey, what about in the toilet stalls?

VIOLET. I don't think that's a proper–

MYRAH. Look, long as Josie's not here, we stick that "OUT OF ORDER" sign on the end stall. Clare shows up, Winifred gets in there real quick. Locks the door. Stands up on the toilet seat, till she leaves. Simple.

WINIFRED. I don't think so.

MYRAH. Rather go to the dogs?

WINIFRED. Nooo.

VIOLET. What does your sister look like, dear?

WINIFRED. Rather frightening. I mean, she's bigger than me. Older. Stronger.

MYRAH. Yeah, but how would we recognize her. Horns? Fangs?

WINIFRED. No. Red hair. Glasses. Real thick ones. A dog whistle around her neck. And– white rabbit shoes.

VIOLET. Rabbit shoes?

WINIFRED. Well, you see, she used to have the dogs chase this stuffed rabbit, on wheels. Then she hit on the idea of making rabbit skin shoes, so the dogs would follow her.

MYRAH. Sounds like she's got more problems than you. Well, we'll get rid of her. All you gotta do is get in that toilet stall, real quick, and keep still.

WINIFRED. My canaries– I couldn't hold onto the cage. I don't want her seeing them.

MYRAH. Here, I'll just stick them under the desk. Throw my fur jacket over them.

(**MYRAH** *covers cage with her fur*)

WINIFRED. Can they get enough air? Birds need lots of fresh air.

MYRAH. Hey, this fur's got so many moth holes, an elephant could breathe through it.

(*SOUND*)

VIOLET. Here comes somebody.

(*all come to attention like pointer setters*)

WINIFRED. (*relaxing*) No, that's not her.

(**PATRON # 6**, *in a brown coat and white shoes, walks through to washroom. She's carrying a boom box and wearing huge red earphones.*)

VIOLET. No rabbit shoes.

MYRAH. *(barking like a dog, no response)* No dog training either.

WINIFRED. Wait, I have my bird watching binoculars. Maybe one of you could keep a lookout, watch that hallway?

VIOLET. I'll stand guard, Winifred.

(**VIOLET** *takes binoculars and stands importantly at the doorway post, surveying the long hall. Music is heard in distance.*)

MYRAH. What the hell's that noise?

WINIFRED. It sounds like marching music.

(**PATRON # 6** *walks out of washroom. They watch her curiously as if music were emanating from her.*)

MYRAH. *(goes to window)* Shoulda known– The May Day parade! Coming right down Main Street.

WINIFRED. Henry marched away to music like that.

(**VIOLET** *uses binoculars out the window and down hall alternately. The music gets steadily louder.*)

VIOLET. Just look at Old Glory waving!

MYRAH. Here, let's get this window open wider. Like a convent they keep us.

(struggle to open the window wider)

WINIFRED. All those young men in uniform–

VIOLET. Daddy always took me to every parade. I'd sit on his shoulders….

(rhythmatically marches in place as she "da dums")

MYRAH. Wowee!! Look at all those handsome men. Some peaches!

WINIFRED. I just hope they come back. I just hope every one of them returns from the wars.

MYRAH. Wars? They ain't going no place, Winifred. Just

down Main Street and back.

VIOLET. Here comes the cavalry! Would you care to share the glasses, Myrah?

MYRAH. Nah. I think I'll just go out on this little balcony. Get me a better view. Can't see much of Main Street from this here alley window.

(**MYRAH** *takes off her shoes, climbs onto the window bench, and struggles to get through the window.*)

Here goes! Geroninmo!

VIOLET. Careful.

MYRAH. *(stands outside window, shouting)* Yoo hoo! Helloo there boys! Helloo!! Show them who's loyal! Give em hell, you sons of guns!

VIOLET. My, her voice really carries.

(*now there's just rhythmatic drum beats*)

MYRAH. Left! Right! I had a good home– I left– you're right!

(**MYRAH** *continues shouting in distance, going around corner of the balcony, out of sight*)

VIOLET. *(turns from window)* Why Winifred dear, you're crying.

WINIFRED. All those men in uniform. I keep thinking of my Henry.

VIOLET. He'll come back dear, don't worry.

WINIFRED. It's been forty years– and no word.

VIOLET. There still could be.

WINIFRED. It's not working anymore. Trying to stay exactly as I was on our wedding day. I looked at my wedding photo this morning. I don't look like that anymore.

VIOLET. Well, he probably looks different too.

WINIFRED. Two weeks– that's all we had– out of a whole lifetime.

VIOLET. You're fortunate. Some people never even have that.

WINIFRED. Mercy, look how dark the sky's getting.

VIOLET. Wilbur, the Weather Man, he predicts rain.

(Drums fade in the distance. **MYRAH** *pokes head in window.)*

MYRAH. Damn short parade, if you ask me. Not like they used to be. *(Starts climbing in.)* Little help please, legs ain't what they used to be either.

*(***WINIFRED*** *and* **VIOLET** *help her in. Pettipants and stockings catch on protrusion.)*

Oops! Always something grabbing at my legs.

WINIFRED. Look– Your stockings– all torn.

MYRAH. Worth it. Just to see so many good looking men in one place. Be a honey, get me that scrub pail with some water, huh.

*(***WINIFRED*** *leaves.)*

Pettipants ripped too. Aagh, fix them later.

(takes off pettipants and drapes them over back of chair)

VIOLET. You shouldn't have gone out there, Myrah.

MYRAH. *(huffs as she takes off her stockings)* You gotta meet life halfway, Violet. Go where the action is. Charley, or was it Clarence– Anyways him and me, we used to chase fire engines, ambulances. Sure gave our nights some extra excitement.

*(***WINIFRED*** *returns with pail.)*

WINIFRED. Here you are.

MYRAH. You are one peach. Just soak this muck off my tootsies.

(puts both feet in pail)

Feels good. No shoes. No stockings. No girdle. Let it all hang out!

WINIFRED. *(looking off into space, hands kneading material on her skirt)* I can't go away with Clare.

MYRAH. You feeling okay, Winifred?

WINIFRED. *(walks SL)* My house– I promised Henry– I'd be there, waiting.

VIOLET. Why don't you just rest awhile.

WINIFRED. *(facing front)* I had another house once.... Under the Christmas tree, the most beautiful doll house– Only, during the night– someone smashed it, like a giant foot came down upon it. Clare, face all puffed up, eyes bulging, screamed at me, "I smashed your doll house, because I hate you! Because mama gives you everything! And nobody likes me– because I'm fat and wear glasses." Then she grabbed the ruffle of my new organdy dress, the one mama made me. Tore the dress right off me. I just stood there– didn't say a word.

MYRAH. Don't go getting upset about that again. Past is past.

WINIFRED. I don't want to go with Clare!

MYRAH. You don't have to. We'll see to that.

> *(**PATRON # 7**, elegantly dressed, walks through. **MYRAH** gives a complimentary whistle.)*

WINIFRED. *(brighter mood)* Gracious Henry's plant hasn't been watered all week. I think Josie wants it to die. *(**WINIFRED** goes to the washroom.)*

> *(**MYRAH** takes feet out of pail, wipes with stockings, puts shoes back on)*

VIOLET. I see you don't wear your mail order copper bracelet any more.

MYRAH. Nah. Didn't help the arthritis none. Just ringed my arm in grasshopper green.

VIOLET. Mama always wore a bracelet– pure gold. I'm not sure if I sold it or not.

> *(**WINIFRED** returns with paper cup. Waters plants in several trips.)*

MYRAH. You know, if I had money enough, I'd go sit in one of those empty copper mines. My cousin Rosie, she lives in Nevada, writes she goes down in them once a week.

VIOLET. A copper mine?

MYRAH. Yep. Cures the arthritis. Says it's a good place to

meet older men too. Dark. And everyone looks a hel-
luva lot more romantic down there. *(ponders)* Course, I
don't know if I'd want to hook up with somebody else
who's got arthritis too.

(SOUND)

VIOLET. Oh dear. Oh dear! I think it's her! Bunny shoes,
hopping right this way.

MYRAH. *(jumps into action)* Quick Winifred, into the can!

WINIFRED. *(drops cup)* Clare? What will I do? *(flustered, starts
gathering things)*

MYRAH. *(shoves everything else under sofa skirt)* Just get going
girl! And don't come out till I yell "All clear!"

*(**MYRAH** and **VIOLET** quickly sit, striking innocent
poses. **VIOLET** embroiders. **MYRAH** reads, humming
"Hallelujah I'm a Bum.")*

*(**CLARE** enters with a brisk stride. She wears a brown
uniform-type outfit with "CLARE'S CANINE CAMPUS"
embroidered on the back of the jacket, a silver whistle on
thick cord around her neck, and white fur shoes. She
carries a large umbrella. There is a trailing dog leash
around her waist and an air of authority, a "being
in charge" attitude. Her personality vacillates between
jovial and authoritative. She eyes **MYRAH** and **VIOLET**,
then proceeds to check out the washroom. Sounds of her
whistle, doors slamming. **PATRON #7** rushes out. **CLARE**
starts to exit, then backtracks. She takes a drink from the
water fountain, observes, hesitates, then queries.)*

CLARE. Pardon me–

*(**MYRAH** and **VIOLET** ignore her.)*

(louder) Pardon me, but do you know if Winifred
Dunkel has been here yet this morning?

MYRAH. *(like she's hard of hearing)* Who?

CLARE. Win-i-fred Dun-kel?

MYRAH. I don know. Lots of people come and go here.

CLARE. She's rather thin. Scrawny looking–

MYRAH. *(before she's finished)* Nah, I didn't see her.

VIOLET. *(looking up quickly, then back down)* I didn't either.

(**CLARE** *tries to sit in Center chair.*)

CLARE. *(jovially)* Well, I'll just sit here and wait then.

MYRAH. That seat's saved.

CLARE. For who?

VIOLET. Our friend.

CLARE. Your friend. Ohhh. *(scrutinizes them both, then points umbrella at them, laughing heartily)* Of course, you must be them.

VIOLET. We aren't anybody.

CLARE. You– you're Violet. And you, the heavy one, with the arthritis. Why, she's written me all about you two.

(Clare's umbrella tip is near Myrah's bosom.)

MYRAH. Watch where you're poking that umbrella, bozo.

CLARE. *(authoritative air)* It's very important that I track down my sister.

VIOLET. Poor Winifred hasn't been here in over a week.

MYRAH. Yeah. Probably still sick.

CLARE. Sick? How sick?

MYRAH. Oh, pretty bad. Probably still home in bed.

VIOLET. Or maybe even the hospital.

CLARE. No– I went to her home first. And she won't go near a hospital.

VIOLET. I wonder where she could be.

MYRAH. Probably changed her mind. Went somewhere's else today. *(walks over to window)*

CLARE. No. Winifred never changes her plans. I know her like a book. You see, I had to take care of her when mama took sick all the time. Why, I practically raised her. *(officious again)* I'm very good at training animals– and people.

MYRAH. Well, Winifred don't happen to be no animal, and don't happen to need no training, especially from the likes of you!

(**CLARE** *laughs it off.*)

VIOLET. Why don't you come back later. We'll tell her you were inquiring about her.

CLARE. Time is very important. If I'm not back by four o'clock, my dogs' feeding time, they get fiercely hungry, then they get viscious– attack. And Winifred always dawdles so with her packing.

MYRAH. That your broken down brown van parked in the alley there?

CLARE. Yes, it is.

MYRAH. And you're taking Winifred away in that heap of junk?

CLARE. I really don't think what I do with Winifred is any of your business.

VIOLET. We're her friends. We care what happens to her.

CLARE. (*To* **VIOLET**) Well– I'm taking her– on a vacation.

MYRAH. What if Winifred don't want to go on no vacation?

VIOLET. She enjoys her little home.

CLARE. Two weeks away from that house, and everything in it, will do her a world of good, whether she knows it or not.

MYRAH. I don't think Winifred will want to go away right now, being sick and all that.

VIOLET. Winifred's really a very happy person. Manages quite well by herself.

CLARE. I only know what her letters tell me. Once I see her, then I'll know for sure.

MYRAH. That she should be put away– Then you can take over her house, and–

CLARE. I don't know where you get your misinformation.

VIOLET. She's afraid. You took her mother away, you know.

CLARE. I put mama in a lovly nursing home, and–

(*All of a sudden, birds chirp faintly.*)

What was that?

MYRAH. I didn't hear nothing.

VIOLET. *(quickly)* Neither did I.

CLARE. Sounded like birds. *(rotates head suspiciously)*

MYRAH. Birds?

CLARE. Yes. Canaries.

MYRAH. Did you hear any birds, Violet?

VIOLET. No. I didn't hear any birds. Whatever would canaries be doing in a rest room?

(Birds twitter again.)

CLARE. Those are birds, all right. *(poking umbrella into corners, behind plants)* They're hiding here somewhere.

MYRAH. Radiator– makes chirping sounds sometimes.

VIOLET. Yes. Yes, it does.

MYRAH. Ladies in the can make strange noises too.

(CLARE uncovers cage, lifts it up, birds twitter)

CLARE. Winifred's birds! I'd know this cage anywhere.

VIOLET. You're scaring the birdies.

(CLARE sets birds on desk, contemplates)

CLARE. Up to her old hide and seek games. *(laughs)* But, she forgets– Clare always finds her. Always.

MYRAH. Find her someplace else then, huh.

CLARE. As a child, we had to keep her in a harness, tied to the clothesline, because she was always running away.

MYRAH. From you, I bet.

CLARE. Every Saturday, she'd run off to Rosenblooms. Mama always sent me to find her. I know all her hiding places here.

(Big splashing noise is heard from the washroom.)
What was that?

MYRAH. Nothing. Old store. Faulty toilets.

VIOLET. *(urgently)* You'd better keep on with your search. You can see she's not here.

CLARE. First thing, I'll notify the security guards, at all the doors.

MYRAH. I wouldn't do that, if I was you. Winifred ain't no criminal– Or runaway dog.

CLARE. *(tapping her umbrella on floor for emphasis)* My sister needs help!

MYRAH. Not from you, she don't. People aren't animals! They don't need keepers. They need somebody to show them the joys of life– *(tries to do an exotic twirl)*

CLARE. I think you might need some help too.

MYRAH. Listen sister, I don't need anybody's help! I been on my own since I was twelve, and I'll be on my own till the day I die! And I'll fight anybody who tries to tell me or Winifred or anybody else how to run our lives –

CLARE. I don't have time to stay here and listen to your stupid babble.

MYRAH. Nobody's asking you to. So get going!

CLARE. I'll be back! You can count on that. *(goes to pick up bird cage)*

MYRAH. You leave that bird cage right where it is!

CLARE. These birds are going with me!

(**MYRAH** *whacks her cane down sharply on the desk next to the bird cage.)*

MYRAH. Oh no they're not!

(**CLARE** *whacks her umbrella down with equal force next to the cane.)*

CLARE. Oh yes they are!

MYRAH. Keep away from those birds! *(threatens with cane)*

CLARE. You don't order me around! *(threatens with umbrella)*

MYRAH. And NOBODY orders me around!

(grabs umbrella away and throws it to doorway, lifts cane)

Maybe you need some special animal training. Like a good caning on your fat behind.

CLARE. You touch me with that thing and I'll file criminal assault charges against you!

MYRAH. Them's fighting words. War time now!

(quickly puts pettipants onto cane end and raises it up as a flag)

And this is gonna be our banner– Flag! Semper Fi

Delis! Charge!

(**CLARE** *tears pettipants off cane tip as* **MYRAH** *charges at her.*)

CLARE. Take– your– dirty– filthy– rag–

(**CLARE** *throws pettipants down on the floor and begins stomping on it.*)

MYRAH. Watch it, sister, that's U.S. Marine property your bunny boots are stomping on!

(**MYRAH** *picks up pettipants, shaking them in* **CLARE**'s *face*)

Go on, get out of here before Semper Fidelis starts waving permanently from around your neck!

CLARE. *(as she exits)* Now I know for sure Winifred has to get away. Not only from her house– and plants– and birds, but from the two of you too!

(**CLARE** *picks up umbrella and exits through doorway.*)

VIOLET. You certainly made her angry.

(**MYRAH** *sits and puts pettipants back on, pinning them together with large safety pin.*)

MYRAH. Yeah, what do you think she did to me?

VIOLET. Well, you did provoke her a bit.

MYRAH. Reminded me of my old man. Laughing like a hyena one minute, mean as the devil the next. Beat the hell out of ma– little mouse of a woman. Laughing while he did it…. Now, what am I thinking of that crap for. Past is past.

VIOLET. Winifred– she's still standing in there.

MYRAH. Oh yeah, Winifred. Almost forgot about her. *(yells)* All clear!

VIOLET. What do we do now?

MYRAH. Wait. Till Miss Bunny Two Shoes hops back to her dogs.

VIOLET. She certainly seemed determined to take Winifred.

MYRAH. Yeah, well I'm just as determined Winifred ain't going away!

(There's a wailing sound, and **WINIFRED** *staggers out of the washroom, carrying her shoes. The bottom half of her is dripping wet.)*

MYRAH & VIOLET. Winifred!

MYRAH. My god! What happened?

WINIFRED. *(wailing)* I fell in!

VIOLET. Poor dear!

WINIFRED. My legs– they just gave out– and I crumpled right into the bowl.

*(**PATRON # 8** walks in. Looks at scene in puzzlement.)*

MYRAH. Whatsa matter lady, you never seen someone what fell in the toilet before?

(QUICK CURTAIN)

End of Scene 1

Scene Two

(About a half hour later. **VIOLET** *is still watching the hallway with binoculars.* **MYRAH** *is at window.)*

MYRAH. Rain clouds still circling above, and that dog van still squatting below.

*(***PATRON # 9*** *walks in.* **MYRAH** *blocks washroom door with arms.)* Sorry honey, someone's dressing in there. *(***PATRON # 9*** *sits impatiently with legs crossed.)*

VIOLET. She'll be out soon, miss. Just changing her wet wedding dress. *(sits in chair, still using binoculars)*

MYRAH. Remind me tomorrow, I gotta apply for another senior citizen card. Hate that place. Stand in line. Fill out forms. All government offices are alike. Lucky I don't need food stamps. Starve to death waiting.

VIOLET. I went there once, I think it was there, to apply for a job.

MYRAH. Yeah, me too. Nobody ever called. And I'll be damned if I do housework. Clean up somebody's else's dirt.

VIOLET. It seems they always want someone with experi- ence– or someone younger.

MYRAH. Yeah, think after sixty we don't have to eat.

VIOLET. I always thought I'd like to teach dancing....

MYRAH. This one time, I was gonna make a mint, teach Rags to sing. Sent for this talking dog record. Musta played it a couple hundred times.

VIOLET. Did it work?

MYRAH. Nah. Not with Rags. But me, I could sing like a dog real good.

(howls to Jingle Bells)

VIOLET. How is little Doggie? You haven't brought him down here for awhile.

MYRAH. Aagh, you know how Josie's about animals in her precious rest room. He's getting pretty old. Hind leg's crippled up. Can't hardly see. But, there's life in him yet. Nough to keep my feet warm at night. Hate sleeping alone, and a dog's better'n nothing.

(**WINIFRED** *enters carrying her dress, wearing a gold cape.*)

WINIFRED. It's still damp, so I'll just hang it here. I want it fresh for the zoo. (*drapes dress over green chair*)

MYRAH. Okay lady, you may now enter.

(*She steps aside with bowing gesture.* **PATRON #9** *rushes in.*)

Let me get you a dress box, Winifred. Some dodo might just decide to sit there.

(**MYRAH** *exits.*)

WINIFRED. (*at window*) Maybe I won't even get to the zoo today.

VIOLET. Don't always worry so, child.

(**VIOLET** *goes to her, stands with her hands clasped, and recites brightly, as a memorized school piece.*)

"It's easy enough to be pleasant–
When life flows by like a song–
But the man worthwhile– Is the man–

(*has trouble remembering*)

Is the man– Who will– smile–
When everything goes dead wrong.
For– the test of the heart– (*can't remember*)
–The test of the heart–

(*gives up with a weak smile*) Where did all those words go? I used to know every one of them.

WINIFRED. Clouds everywhere now. It's never rained on my anniversary.

VIOLET. Did you have a nice wedding day?

WINIFRED. (*moving away, remembering*) Beautiful! Warm. Sunshiney. Sparklingest day of my life.

VIOLET. I would have picked May too, not June. If I'd gotten married.

WINIFRED. –And the birds, they just filled Honeysuckle

Park with their lilting songs of joy.

VIOLET. –Mama always said, if I got married, we'd have a garden wedding. Under our old weeping willow. *(pause)* Garden's all weeds now. Willow's been dead for years.

*(**MYRAH** returns with a huge dress box.)*

MYRAH. Young snit wanted to know what I wanted a dress box for.

*(As **PATRON # 9** leaves washroom, she opens her purse for a tissue to blow her nose and drops a $20 bill as she exits.)*

*(**MYRAH** picks it up, goes to door)*

MYRAH. *(shouting)* Hey lady, you dropped something. *(shrugs)* Twenty bucks! Well, can't run after her, not with this bum leg.

(stuffs it down her bosom, sits, winces in pain)

Feels worse. Good thing I'm seeing Doc Brummer again this Friday.

VIOLET. Some new ailment?

MYRAH. Nah. Just my six month checkup. See that all my female organs are still in good shape.

(folds dress up into box)

VIOLET. Oh.

MYRAH. Once they go, you can start packing for the fox farm.

VIOLET. I certainly wouldn't know what to pack. *(titters)*

MYRAH. He's some doc, even if he is Medicare. Little old, but when those experienced hands start feeling me. Boy, I still get shivers up and down the old spine. Other places too. You should see a doc, Winifred, all that sickness you got.

WINIFRED. No. I– don't go to doctors. Not anymore.

MYRAH. Oh yeah, I forgot.

WINIFRED. Ever since– Robin–

MYRAH. That's okay, Winifred, you don't have to repeat

that sad tale again.

WINIFRED. Nine months I carried her. Henry's and my child....

VIOLET. Maybe you better not.

WINIFRED. The sky was black. Just like now. Then the pain began. *(begins breathing heavily)* I called out for Henry, over and over. Clare kept holding me down. Then– Robin began to be born, and– and– *(breathing more difficult)* Clare ran out– to get a doctor, she said, leaving me all alone– screaming. *(stops, is slower, more vague)* I don't remember what happened after– The whole world went blank for three days. *(crying)* I never even saw little Robin. Clare said something was wrong with her– She wouldn't have lived anyway.

VIOLET. Don't go on, dear.

WINIFRED. They put me in this terrifying hospital after. All those strange men in white.... *(softly)* I don't go to doctors anymore.

VIOLET. You shouldn't have told us again. Upset yourself so.

MYRAH. *(gets up, claps hands)* Come on ladies, this ain't no funeral parlor. Spring's just around the corner.

(goes into song and dance)

"Pack up your troubles in your old kit bag,

And smile, smile, smile– "

(Myrah's leg gives out with last kick, wincing in pain)

Damn leg. Maybe some cold water'll help. Keep a watch for that Clare, huh.

*(**MYRAH** exits to washroom.)*

WINIFRED. *(noticing lilacs, vaguely)* Are the lilacs in bloom already?

VIOLET. I picked those from mama's bush, just this morning.

*(**WINIFRED** walks to window. They are each in their own little world.)*

WINIFRED. Daffodils– I carried daffodils for my wedding. Henry said they were little stars of sunshine that would brighten our whole world.

VIOLET. –For my debut, our third floor ballroom was filled with fresh lilac boughs. Perfumed the whole house.

WINIFRED. –That first spring I planted daffodils all around our bungalow – five hundred.

VIOLET. –And I wore this lovely gown of lilac chiffon. From Paris....

WINIFRED. –They keep doubling each year. There must be thousands of daffodils surrounding our bungalow now.

VIOLET. –And I had violets twined in my long brown hair. And when I danced – it was like a halo of purple stars. (VIOLET *twirls a bit*)

WINIFRED. Some days, it's like I'm drowning in a sea of soft yellow daffodils....

VIOLET. That was the loveliest day of my life....

(WINIFRED *picks up the bird cage and wanders back to window.*)

WINIFRED. *(singing strangely, as if to birds)* "It isn't raining rain, you know, it's raining daffodils." You like fresh air, don't you, Romeo. Oh, don't try to open the cage– we're not at home. Romeo! Come back here, Romeo!

(WINIFRED *starts climbing through window, bird cage in hand.*)

(MYRAH *comes out of washroom, sees* WINIFRED *going through the window.*)

MYRAH. Hey, Winifred, don't go out there!

WINIFRED. Romeo– I have to go whistle him back.

VIOLET. Get her back inside, please.

MYRAH. She'll be okay. Those old canaries can't hardly even fly anymore.

WINIFRED. *(whistling and gently calling)* Romeo– Romeo–

VIOLET. Oh dear! I see red hair, and rabbit shoes!

MYRAH. Geez, no time to get Winifred back in. Quick, Violet, shut the window!

VIOLET. But–

MYRAH. Don't argue, just do it!

(*Hurriedly, they shut window as* **CLARE** *enters. She quickly searches the washroom, blowing whistle.*)

(**MYRAH** *begins exercising near window, trying to touch floor.*)

MYRAH. One and two, and–

(**VIOLET** *fusses with plants.*)

CLARE. (*clears throat*) Ladies, I came back– just to check, once more.

VIOLET. Winifred's not here– not here at all.

CLARE. Her bird cage– it's gone.

MYRAH. And so is she! Hard of hearing?

CLARE. I searched every inch of these three floors.

MYRAH. Men's dressing rooms too?

CLARE. Well, the guard is instructed to hold her. If she comes in or out. He has her photo, little old, but–

MYRAH. They got no legal reason to hold Winifred.

CLARE. Stores are very careful these days about letting "suspected shoplifters" enter or exit.

MYRAH. You mean, you told them–

(*faint distant roll of thunder*)

CLARE. What was that!

MYRAH. Little thunder.

VIOLET. Angels– playing ten pins.

CLARE. I certainly hope Winifred's not out there. She's frightened to death of storms.

VIOLET. So many things frighten her.

CLARE. (*laughing at memory*) When she was little, first rumble of thunder, she'd run screaming into mama's bed. Hide under the covers.

VIOLET. I did the same thing.

CLARE. One time, when mama was sick, she tried that with me. I pushed her right out of the bed.

MYRAH. Bet no one's tried to get in bed with you since.

(Rapping on window is heard. **MYRAH** *starts rapping on desk, as if playing piano and humming to drown out sound.)*

CLARE. What's that?

VIOLET. More thunder?

CLARE. No, sounds like knocking– outside the–

MYRAH. Awning– flaps feal funny sometimes.

CLARE. Very strange. (*sees Winifred's bag*)

VIOLET. Yes, very strange.

CLARE. That's Winifred's gold carry bag, isn't it? Hauls Henry's letters around with her all the time. Well, I'll just take it along.

MYRAH. *(lifts cane threateningly)* You leave that bag alone!

VIOLET. Those letters are all she has left.

CLARE. Henry's never coming back!

VIOLET. Winifred believes he will.

CLARE. Well, I received the telegram.

MYRAH. Yeah, she told us 'bout the telegram. "Missing in–

CLARE. That was the first one. I think it's time Winifred read the second one again.

*(**CLARE** takes telegram from jacket pocket.)*

MYRAH. No way are we going to let that happen.

(All of a sudden a heavy downpour begins.)

VIOLET. Oh dear lord, look, a regular cloudburst out there!

CLARE. My van! Windows are wide open. I'll be right back.

*(**CLARE** exits. Loud crash of thunder. Frantic knocking on window.)*

VIOLET. Winifred– we better get her back inside!

MYRAH. Yeah, she's pounding like a maniac now. Damn thing's stuck again. Come on, you S.O.B.!

*(**MYRAH** whacks frame sharply. Window finally opens.)*

WINIFRED. *(stands drenched, holding bird cage, blubbering hysterically.)* Let me in! Oh, please, let me in!

*(**MYRAH** and **VIOLET** help her in and close window. She*

stands dazed and hysterical on window bench.)

VIOLET. I think we better take Winifred home.

MYRAH. Give up? Why, we've just begun to fight.

WINIFRED. I couldn't find the window!

VIOLET. There, there, child. Let me take this bird cage and your dripping cape. You can slip into my coat.

(**VIOLET** *puts purple coat on* **WINIFRED**, *drapes cape over chair)*

WINIFRED. I don't want to play hide and seek anymore.

(collapses in chair)

MYRAH. Guess we can't send her back out there. Find some other place– A dry one.

VIOLET. There is no other place.

MYRAH. I'll think of something.

VIOLET. You're not a magician, Myrah. Even you can't make Winifred just– disappear.

MYRAH. Violet, get me that "OUT OF ORDER" sign.

VIOLET. Whatever for?

MYRAH. Don't question, just get it.

(**WINIFRED** *takes her bag and medicine bottle and sits under the plant.)*

WINIFRED. I'm not going back in that toilet stall again!

(takes drink from medicine bottle and sinks to floor)

VIOLET. Of course not, dear.

(starts going over to **WINIFRED***)*

MYRAH. Violet! Get that sign. Now!

(**VIOLET** *goes to washroom)*

WINIFRED. I'm not moving from this spot. Whomever finds me, wins.

VIOLET. Here's the sign, but whatever–

MYRAH. *(rummaging through purse)* Let's see, eyebrow pencil should work. *(writes in large letters)* CLOSED! FOR REPAIRS!!

VIOLET. Who's closed for repairs?

MYRAH. We are.

(**MYRAH** *leaves.*)

VIOLET. *(calling after, as she gathers things)* I'm sorry Myrah, but– I have to leave.

(*door slams in distance, thunder,* **MYRAH** *returns*)

Let me out Myrah, I have important– other things– to take care of today.

(**MYRAH** *shuts entrance door forcefully and bolts it.*)

MYRAH. What's more important than taking care of Winifred? Selling that doll?

WINIFRED. *(up to* **VIOLET***, clinging.)* Don't leave, Violet.

VIOLET. I don't like being involved in these kinds of upsetting situations.

MYRAH. Who does? I got better things to do too.

WINIFRED. Please stay– till Clare's gone.

MYRAH. Once Clare sees that "CLOSED" sign, she'll give up and head for her hounds.

WINIFRED. Shut doors won't do it. Clare will still know we're here, and she'll bring in the authorities.

VIOLET. I don't want trouble with authorities.

MYRAH. Relax, both of you. Just let me handle things. I got plenty of experience with trouble.

WINIFRED. I think I'll just lie down a bit. My head feels funny. *(lies on window bench)*

VIOLET. Melissa and I were going to have a picnic in Arcadia Park. But, now with this storm–

MYRAH. So– have your dolly picnic right here.

VIOLET. I did promise her.

(*sets out picnic things on coffee table*)

Would you care to join us? Just cucumber sandwiches, caminolle tea– and my last jar of gooseberry preserves.

MYRAH. Nah, I'm on this new diet. No gooseberries. Gonna check over yesterday's Tribune. See if any of my "Letters to the Editor" got in.

VIOLET. *(sets out doll)* We're going to have our picnic inside,

Melissa. Won't that be fun?

MYRAH. *(still half reading paper)* You got no phone calls to make today? Time to kill while we're waiting.

VIOLET. I was going to call– about my electricity bill.

MYRAH. Yeah, and what're you gonna tell them?

VIOLET. Well, I thought, if I explained–

MYRAH. Explaining don't do no good. They got machines answering their phones. Machines don't listen to people's troubles.

VIOLET. I could pay my bill, all my bills, if– when I sell Melissa. *(picks up doll, holds her wistfully)*

MYRAH. Well, you won't be selling her today no more.

VIOLET. I suppose not. They write they're going to shut off the electricity, May fifteenth.

MYRAH. They'd do it too, those bastards. Did it to me a coupla times.

VIOLET. I thought, maybe, during the summer, when it's light for so long, I might not need any electricity.

MYRAH. Girl, you need lights.

VIOLET. Melissa and I go to bed very early.

MYRAH. That neighborhood especially! You should leave lights burning night and day.

VIOLET. I know, but–

MYRAH. Even prisoners get lights. Plus television!

VIOLET. Television. My picture burned out, but I still get sound. Once in awhile, when it gets too terribly lonesome, I turn it on, just listen to the stories.

(loud crash of thunder, birds twitter)

WINIFRED. *(jumps up, screaming)* Mama! Help! The lightning– it's going to get me!

VIOLET. *(goes to comfort her, Melissa in her arms)* It's all right, Winifred.

WINIFRED. *(realizing where she is)* I'm sorry– I forgot where I was. *(rubs eyes, notices Melissa)* Where– did that beautiful doll come from?

VIOLET. This is Melissa. Melissa, my friend, Winifred.

MYRAH. Yep, that's the beauty Violet's selling. To keep the wolf away from her mansion door.

WINIFRED. Don't sell her. She's too lovely. May I hold her?

VIOLET. *(hands Melissa to* **WINIFRED***)* Careful. You can sing to her too. She enjoys that.

(**WINIFRED** *takes doll, sits on window bench, rocks and sings,* **VIOLET** *clears away picnic)*

WINIFRED. "Hush little baby, don't you cry–
Papa's gonna be here bye and bye– "
(stops, hands doll back) Here, you take her. *(turns, staring out window)*

VIOLET. *(sets Melissa on desk chair, facing front.)* Come Melissa, you can sit out for awhile.

(rhythmic rap on door)

WINIFRED. It's her! I know that knock!

(knock again)

MYRAH. *(motions all to be quiet)* Shhhh–

CLARE. Open this door! I know you two are still in there!
(knocks again)

WINIFRED. She won't go away. She won't.

CLARE. I'll report you all to the authorities!

VIOLET. Myrah, this has gone far enough.

CLARE. That homemade sign on that other door didn't fool me one bit.

MYRAH. *(imitates man's voice, uses heavy accent, but no particular nationality)* Sorry lady, daa toilets dey overflow. Floor's all filled mit da water. Place closed for rest of da day.

(**WINIFRED** *and* **VIOLET** *gather near, suppressing mirth at* **MYRAH** *'s character disguise.)*

CLARE. If those two crackerbrained dames put you up to this, I'll see that you lose your job!

MYRAH. Violet, the scrub pail. *(man's voice again)* Toilet water all over da floor, lady. She still overflowing.

(VIOLET gets pail MYRAH soaked feet in. MYRAH pours it under door.)

CLARE. What the devil! Water's coming through the door. All over my bunny shoes!

(All three are standing near door giggling. When WINIFRED hears "bunny shoes," she twirls in a delighted dance.)

WINIFRED. *(sing-song child rhyme)*
"The water ruined her bunny shoes! Bunny shoes–
For Ransy Tansi Ti-I-OO."

(WINIFRED knocks into chair where Melissa is. Doll falls to floor crying.)

VIOLET. *(a passionate cry, as she reaches out too late)* Melissa! Oh dear Lord, my Melissa!
(kneels and gathers doll to her, crying)
My poor, poor baby.

WINIFRED. *(loudly)* I'm sorry!

CLARE. I heard you Winifred, now you're all going to be sorry.

WINIFRED. Ninny Winny. Ninny Winny.

(WINIFRED goes to tall plant, crunches up in a ball-like huddle.)

VIOLET. *(still on floor, caressing doll)* She's broken, mama. All broken. *(rocks back and forth)* Gone…. They're all gone now.

CLARE. One last chance to open this door peacefully. One! Two! Three!
(silence, except Violet's sobs)
Okay, I'm going to the manager himself! *(voice trails off)*

VIOLET. She doesn't even say "Mama" anymore.

WINIFRED. *(resignation in her voice)* Open the door, Myrah.

MYRAH. *(picks up her cane)* What's the matter with you two!

Giving up the first time there's a little trouble. "When the going gets rough, the tough get going!"

WINIFRED. I want to give up.

MYRAH. Well, I don't give up, not without a damn good fight.

VIOLET. I don't care to fight. Not ever. And especially not now.

WINIFRED. I just want to rest.

MYRAH. *(raps cane sharply on table)* Rest! This ain't no time to rest. Why, in England, during the war, those people went through a hell of a lot worse times than these. Did they give up? Not on your life! Every time a bomb fell, they ran out there, put it out! And they're living today, enjoying life, *because* they didn't give in, sit down and cry, when things got a little rough.

VIOLET. One by one, they take everything from us.

MYRAH. You fight back, Violet.

WINIFRED. I could never fight any thing, or any one.

MYRAH. Well, you're gonna start today!

(**MYRAH** *goes to* **VIOLET**, *gently takes the doll from her.*)

Let that dolly rest now, you two can help me.

VIOLET. Nothing more we can do.

MYRAH. You can start shoving, that's what you can do. We'll begin with the desk.

(**MYRAH** *begins shoving the desk in front of the outer door. Momentum picks up from here on.*)

WINIFRED. Josie gave strict orders, not to move the furniture around anymore.

MYRAH. To hell with Josie! We're gonna repeat history.

VIOLET. *(out of her reverie)* We are?

MYRAH. Come on! Let's go! In England, during the blitzkriegs– they piled up everything they could in front of the doors of those flimsy bomb shelter.

VIOLET. Whatever for?

MYRAH. To keep the war on the other side. *And* we're gonna do the same thing for Clare.

WINIFRED. You mean—

MYRAH. Yep, we're gonna blockade the rest room!

VIOLET. I don't think—

MYRAH. Don't think, Violet! Just get a move on and start helping.

VIOLET. But—

MYRAH. Do something for once, girl! Start fighting back! They won't know what hit 'em –

WINIFRED. We'll just get in more trouble.

MYRAH. Stop your whining and start pushing.

VIOLET. *(stands up, goes over to help, new spirit)* All right. I haven't got anything more to lose anyway.

MYRAH. That's the spirit, Violet! This is our rest room. We have a right to protect it against the invaders.

WINIFRED. *(confused)* War? Are we declaring war?

MYRAH. You bet! And it's about time!

> *(They shove the desk in front of the door.)*

Okay. Next the candy machine.

WINIFRED. We're not strong enough for that large machine.

MYRAH. You're always lots stronger than you think you are.
> *(They begin shoving the candy machine.)*

WINIFRED. I never thought I'd be celebrating my anniversary like this.

MYRAH. Celebrate after Clare's gone. That'll really be something to whoop about.

> *(With great abandon, **MYRAH** pulls all handles out on the candy machine. Coins begin clattering into the chute.)*

> *(birds twitter, thunder)*

VIOLET. This was always such a peaceful place. I always stopped here to rest.

> *(**MYRAH** grabs coins that have fallen into the chute. She flings them into air.)*

MYRAH. *(joyfully)* Rest when you're in the cemetery, girl.

While you still got an ounce of breath in you– live!

(bangs machine with her fist)

And fight! Cause once you stop that fight, you might as well be dead!

(whacks machine again with her cane)

Charge!

(Machine begins sputtering out candies.)

VIOLET. Good heavens! Look! Look at all the Lifesavers!

MYRAH. I'll be damned! I hit the jackpot for once!

*(**WINIFRED**, confused, jumps up on window bench as Lifesavers continue pouring out.)*

WINIFRED. Somebody– somebody help us! We're going to be drowned in Lifesavers!!

(QUICK CURTAIN)

End of Act I

ACT II

Scene One

(Short time later. Furniture is piled haphazardly in front of closed door. Three center chairs, now spread further apart. Coffee table and window bench remain. Thunder rumbles in background at opening, then only when indicated. **MYRAH & VIOLET** *struggle to upend the settee.* **WINIFRED** *strains to deposit small potted plant atop the pile.)*

WINIFRED. Up we go.

MYRAH. *(collapsing in chair)* And down we go. Ain't nobody gonna get through that pile of junk.

VIOLET. I just hope we don't get into any trouble.

MYRAH. Worry– worry– that's all you two do. Least helped you forget about that broken doll.

WINIFRED. I'm sorry, Violet, I–

MYRAH. Yeah, well being sorry don't help that doll none. How's Violet gonna pay her light bill now?

VIOLET. *(picks up doll)* Only her face is cracked. Maybe, she could be mended.

MYRAH. Sure, might patch her up. But couldn't sell her like that.

VIOLET. *(brightens)* That's true, isn't it.

MYRAH. Nah. Nobody wants broken stuff today. Crippled things. Old people.

VIOLET. It's all so very clear. Melissa didn't want to leave her cozy home, so she got herself broken, on purpose.

WINIFRED. I kept trying to tell you, then everything got so mixed up. I'll pay you for the doll.

VIOLET. No dear, it was an accident.

MYRAH. Sooo– lots of people collect on accidents. Now, if I had this bum leg from an accident, stead of the damn arthritis, could make a few bucks on the suffering.

WINIFRED. I could give you– ten dollars a month. From my– government checks.

MYRAH. Government checks? What kind you getting?

WINIFRED. Well, the– the government calls it– a war widow pension. *(quickly)* But, it's my allotment from Henry. Like he used to send me every month.

MYRAH. Still takes care of you, huh. Forty years he's gone and that check still keeps coming. I shoulda been so lucky.

VIOLET. We can discuss this another time. Right now my thoughts aren't quite together.

(VIOLET gets up and walks about.)

WINIFRED. Everything's different today. Even this room– furniture swirled around. Nobody walking through. I don't like being closed in.

MYRAH. *(walking about)* Reminds me of the time we were evicted– furniture piled up on the sidewalk. Know what we did to keep away the glooms?

VIOLET. Pray?

MYRAH. Nah. We'd sing.

VIOLET. I don't particularly feel like singing.

(rumble of thunder)

WINIFRED. *(cringing)* Neither do I.

MYRAH. When times was bad, Charley and me, we'd sing up a storm. He had this old gypsy mandolin. Me, a tambourine. Talk about good times. *(Rummaging through her bags.)*

VIOLET. Sunday nights, I'd play the organ– mama the zither, and we'd all sing hymns. I forget when I sold the organ– or what happened to that zither.

MYRAH. Hymns you want, hymns you'll get. Perfectly good song book, woman next door threw out. What about "Bringing in the Sheaves"? *(stands up)* Okay, all together now.

(**MYRAH** *begins singing, directing with her hands. Her voice isn't that great, but it's loud and strong.*)

"Sowing in the morning, sowing seeds of kindness– "

(*Slowly* **VIOLET & WINIFRED** *stand and join in, as song takes on bit more joyous tones.*)

MYRAH & VIOLET & WINIFRED.

"Sowing in the moontide and the dewey eve;
Waiting for the harvest and the time of reaping,
We shall come rejoicing, bringing in the sheaves."

CLARE. (*pounding on door and shouting*) Winifred! Winifred!

(*Group stops singing, look at one another, hesitating.* **MYRAH** *motions them to keep going. They continue even stronger. Thunder, birds, and* **CLARE**'s *pounding concur simultaneously.*)

MYRAH & VIOLET & WINIFRED.

"Bringing in the sheaves– Bringing in the sheaves,
We shall come rejoicing, bringing in the sheaves."

CLARE. That's it! I'm going to get the janitor.

(*Second of silence, then all sing again, even stronger.*)

MYRAH & VIOLET & WINIFRED.

"Sowing in the sunshine, sowing in the shadows,
Fearing neither clouds nor winter's chilling breeze;
By and by the harvest, and the labor ended– "

CLARE. (*voice trailing off*) You'll be sorry, Winifred.

MYRAH & VIOLET & WINIFRED. (*singing dies halfheartedly*)

"We shall come rejoicing–
Bringing in– the– sheaves."

VIOLET. It's not the same– singing in a rest room.

WINIFRED. I only feel worse. Maybe some more medicine. (**WINIFRED** *goes to washroom with her bag*)

VIOLET. Myrah, if Clare goes for the janitor–

MYRAH. Won't find him. Joe's always at the races on Monday.

VIOLET. Winifred does not look well, nor sound well. If she needs a doctor, how could one even get in here?

MYRAH. You heard her– "No more doctors!"

VIOLET. Well, something's wrong with her. Door blocked up, no way for fresh air to get in.

MYRAH. Look, if air's bad, her birds croak first. Miners always take canaries down to test for bad air.

VIOLET. Such a pity if anything happened to her birds.

(**WINIFRED** *re-enters, seems more dazed.*)

WINIFRED. My birds! What's going to happen to my birds?

MYRAH. Nothing's gonna happen to your birds. Nothing's gonna happen to any of us.

(*There's a loud crack of thunder, bright flash of lightning, lights go out, general cries of disorder, the following is simultaneous*)

VIOLET. The lights!

MYRAH. Power line's hit, that's all.

WINIFRED. Romeo! Juliet!

MYRAH. Hang on, I'll get my trusty ever-ready flashlight.

(*falls over coffee table*)

Damn! My good leg too.

WINIFRED. I should never have come out today.

MYRAH. Wouldn't have missed this day for the world.

VIOLET. Here's a candle, and matches.

MYRAH. Good. Batteries pooped again.

WINIFRED. Hurry, I'm afraid in the dark.

(**MYRAH** *lights a vigil light and sets it on the coffee table. Lights glows eerily. There's also faint light from window.*)

MYRAH. Kinda romantic, ain't it. Candlelight. A little wine, some soft music–

(*takes long silky scarf from bag and goes into seductive tango.*)

Da da da– da da da da– da da da– da da da da.

WINIFRED. Myrah, please, you're just making me more nervous.

MYRAH. (*throws scarf down angrily*) Well, for crying– You know what your trouble is, Winifred.

VIOLET. Myrah, she's been ill.

MYRAH. I don't care! I'm sick and tired of people bellyaching. Not wanting anybody else to have any fun.

VIOLET. Please–

MYRAH. *(continuing her tirade)* You know what your trouble is, Winifred! You don't get any fun out of life! Everything's one big, fat serious crisis for you. End of the world! When all it really is– is your head getting stuck in bad times, and–

VIOLET. She's not feeling well–

MYRAH. Well, neither am I! Bet I'm sicker than both of you. But you don't see me going around yammering all the time.

WINIFRED. *(rising)* I think I need to–

MYRAH. Just sit down, Winifred, and shut up!

WINIFRED. *(starts sniffling)* But, I–

MYRAH. Now! *(pacing)* Okay, you didn't want to see your sister. Right? So, we went through a lot of trouble to keep her away. Did we complain? No. But minute a little something goes wrong, you start crying. Want to give up before you even start.

VIOLET. Anyone's who waited forty years, certainly does not give up very easily.

WINIFRED. *(covering face with hands)* I'm sorry, Myrah. I don't know what's wrong with me today.

VIOLET. Here's my handkerchief, dear.

MYRAH. *(letting up, sitting down)* Aagh, forget it. Ain't your fault you still believe all that fairy tale crap. Prince Charming coming along– marrying you. Both living happily ever after. *(looking away, introspective)* Yeah, well, life ain't like that, Winifred. Prince Charming don't always stay charming. And beautiful princesses grow old– and sometimes ugly. *(shrugs)* But, you just gotta make the best of it.

VIOLET. You're not being very kind to Winifred.

MYRAH. Don't think I'm kind, huh?

VIOLET. Well, sometimes you don't use good manners, and–

MYRAH. *(back to her tirade, finger at* **VIOLET.***)* Manners! You know what your trouble is, Violet? You're *too* damn polite! You let people walk all over you, then you thank them for it!

VIOLET. I most certainly–

MYRAH. Pl-eese! No rude interruptions! You're so afraid of going against those phony rules you been taught as a kid, you won't even try nothing new. Well, the world's moved ahead, dearie. All that grace and charm don't work no more. Emily Post's been dead for years, case nobody's told you.

VIOLET. *(anger raising)* Nobody needs to tell me anything.

MYRAH. You're so filled with how you should act, what you should say, you don't even know what your real self would do if it ever got the chance. You could never say 'shit' if you had to.

VIOLET. *(shouts back angrily)* Shit!

MYRAH. Wowie! You ain't never gonna be that same polite Violet anymore.

VIOLET. I don't know– what made me–

MYRAH. Well you said it– and that's that.

WINIFRED. When are the lights coming back on?

MYRAH. Who cares. We ain't going no place. *(pause)* Anybody for a game of Lotto? Got the box right here in my bag– somewhere.

VIOLET. No thank you.

WINIFRED. Everything's so shadowy. Like spirits were hovering.

MYRAH. Now what kind of spirits would want to hang around Rosenblooms? And in the rest room yet?

VIOLET. One time, mama and I, we were at a seance. And I did hear a voice, coming right out of the air. It sounded just like daddy.

MYRAH. Fake. Me and Clarence, we worked that spiritualism stuff. After our burlesque act conked out.

VIOLET. You mean, you're acquainted with calling up spirits? Maybe– I could talk to mama–

WINIFRED. Don't! Once people are dead, it's best to leave them be.

VIOLET. Could you– maybe try?

MYRAH. Been a pretty long time. Connections probably all rusty.

WINIFRED. I'd rather play Lotto.

MYRAH. Just close my eyes a minute. See if anybody's around. *(closes eyes, hands to temple, hums monotone)*

WINIFRED. Myrah, don't!

(All of a sudden, the small plant atop the furniture pile falls to floor with a loud crash. All three scream.)

VIOLET. Good heavens!

WINIFRED. Henry! That was Henry's plant. Could he–

MYRAH. You know, that's just who it might be.

WINIFRED. Oh no!

(loud crash of thunder, eerie beam of flashlight filters through from behind closed hall door)

CLARE. *(in deep man's voice, calling gently)* Winifred! Winifred! Are you in there?

WINIFRED. Henry! Oh dear lord, it's Henry!

*(**WINIFRED** collapses in dead faint.)*

VIOLET. Good heavens, she's dead. Winifred's dead!

MYRAH. She ain't dead. Just fainted. So come over here and help. Slip that pillow under.

*(They prop **WINIFRED** up with the pillow.)*

CLARE. *(knocking, man's voice)* Winifred– are you in there?

MYRAH. Yeah, she's in here, and she's fainted. So cut the bad acting, you over-ripe ham.

CLARE. If my sister needs medical attention, you better let me in!

MYRAH. If your sister needs medical attention, it's because of you! So buzz off!

CLARE. We'll get in there. Soon as the electricity's back on, the janitor's going to drill that lock off.

MYRAH. Yeah, well, there's lots more than the door to get through– *if* you find a janitor.

VIOLET. I have some smelling salts.

MYRAH. Water– get me some water.

(**VIOLET** *takes pail to washroom. Light from window brightens as storm begins to fade.*)

CLARE. The store officials are being notified also.

MYRAH. (*at door*) Aagh. They won't do nothing to us. Know why? Cause they don't want no bad publicity about their precious Rosenblooms. Goldie Blatz, one time, she tried committing suicide down here. Slashed her wrists, right over the end sink. Rosenblooms did everything they could to keep the whole mess quiet.

CLARE. Well, I'll take you to court myself.

MYRAH. Listen sister, ain't nothing you can threaten me with. Cause there ain't that much left for them to take away.

(**MYRAH** *walks away from door.*)

(**VIOLET** *returns with the pail.*)

VIOLET. Here's the water. Difficult seeing in the dark.

MYRAH. Come on, Winifred. Time to wake up.

(**MYRAH** *pours pail. Only few drops come out.*)
Violet!

VIOLET. I didn't want her getting wet all over again.

(*Suddenly lights come back on. Birds begin singing.*)

WINIFRED. (*coming to*) Birds! I hear birds... Am I in heaven?

MYRAH. Nope. Just Rosenblooms rest room.

VIOLET. You fainted dear.

WINIFRED. (*still vague*) Henry– I heard Henry's voice.

MYRAH. Nah, just your sister, with her ham acting.

CLARE. (*trying to maintain calmness*) Winifred!

WINIFRED. It's Clare! She's still out there!

CLARE. If you don't come out quietly, right now, they'll have to come and take you away. Like mama.

WINIFRED. No! *(clinging to* **MYRAH***)*

CLARE. They'll take your house away too.

WINIFRED. *(terrified)* No! No!

> *(***VIOLET** *suddenly takes her umbrella and whacks it against the door)*

VIOLET. *(shouting angrily)* You leave Winifred and her house alone!

CLARE. Open this door, Winifred.

VIOLET. Nobody's opening any door! Winifred is not going anywhere with anyone! We'll stay here all night with her if we have to!

MYRAH. Give it to her, Violet!

VIOLET. *(another whack with umbrella)* You have no right taking anyone out of their house against their will. It's heartless. Destroying all their memories. Treating them as if there wasn't a human spirit inside their body at all. You have to start letting us alone!

> *(one final whack,* **VIOLET** *turns and walks away)*

MYRAH. *(applause)* Bravo!

CLARE. *(blows whistle, commanding)* Don't listen to those blabbering biddies, Winifred. Come to the door–

MYRAH. Will you just cut the noise out there. You sound like a bellowing hound dog in heat.

> *(birds twitter,* **WINIFRED** *goes to calm them)*

CLARE. *(shouting)* Nobody talks to me like that! You big mouthed battleaxe!

MYRAH. Back to your cage, red headed baboon!

CLARE. Back to yours– overdressed hippopotamus!

MYRAH. Oh– go stick your whistle up your ass!

> *(door slams, silence)*

VIOLET. My, the rain's stopped.

MYRAH. Got her to leave, anyway. Think we could use some fresh air right now.

> *(***MYRAH** *opens window, sun spills in)*

WINIFRED. *(walks with bird cage)* We won't be going to the zoo today, Romeo and Juliet. I might have to go away– like mama.

*(**WINIFRED** puts birds down and takes medicine bottle on her way to the washroom.)*

MYRAH. Hey Winifred, leave the medicine here, okay.

*(**MYRAH** takes the bottle from her. There is no resistance. **WINIFRED** goes to the washroom.)*

Look at this will you. Alcohol! Twenty percent! No wonder she acts more goofy when she's sick. Wonder how much of this stuff she carries around with her. *(**MYRAH** starts going through Winifred's bag)*

VIOLET. Myrah, those are her personal things.

MYRAH. Yeah, well right now, she's our personal responsibility. Pressed daffodils. Letters– all tied up with a yellow ribbon.

VIOLET. Don't go through them.

MYRAH. How nosy do you think I am.

VIOLET. Quick, she's coming back.

WINIFRED. I'd like my medicine now, please. It's the only thing that helps my asthma.

*(**WINIFRED** takes the bottle from **MYRAH** and takes a long drink.)*

CLARE. *(calling from down below)* Winifred! Winifred Dunkel!

WINIFRED. Clare! She's looking for me! I've got to hide.

MYRAH. *(to window.)* Good lord, she's down in that alley now, on top of her van.

WINIFRED. *(scurrying about)* I have to get under the porch, so she can't find me.

VIOLET. There's no porch here.

CLARE. Winifred! Come to the window!

WINIFRED. Where's mama? I've got to hide.

*(**WINIFRED** goes to the washroom door.)*

In this closet. Don't tell Clare where I am.

VIOLET. But, that's not–

MYRAH. Let her go, till she calms down anyway. *(quick look out window)* Looks like the Brown Barker's given up anyhow.

VIOLET. Poor child, doesn't even know where she is. I think this has gone far enough, Myrah. Open the doors.

MYRAH. Too late. That bozo's out for blood. Probably on her way to the police station this very minute.

VIOLET. She wouldn't really take us to court, would she?

MYRAH. Damn right. Then make sure we go to jail too.

VIOLET. Jail?

MYRAH. Yep. And I've had enough of those hell holes.

VIOLET. You've been in one?

MYRAH. Aagh, coupla years back already. Assault and battery. Hit my landlady over the head with her own wastebasket. Accused me of going to the incinerator in my nightgown. Meeting her broken down Alex behind the furnace.

VIOLET. They sent you to jail?

MYRAH. Yep. Some of the worst days of my life.

(sits tiredly, all energy seems to have left her)

Don't think I could take being locked up like that anymore. Couldn't fight them either. Not like I used to. *(admittance to herself)* I'm too old– and too tired….

VIOLET. Look!

(All of a sudden Clare's head appears in half opened window.)

MYRAH. My god!

(quickly goes to window, closing it halfway, capturing top half of **CLARE** *as she's trying to climb in)*

VIOLET. What are you doing, Myrah?

MYRAH. Quick, get my scarf!

(pulls side spring tabs, locking them in position)

MYRAH. Window peepers aint' welcome here.

CLARE. You crazy fool! Let me out! *(arms flailing)*

MYRAH. Window's locked. Now tie up her hands.

(**MYRAH** *ties them with her tango scarf.*)

VIOLET. She must have climbed that rickety old fire escape from atop her van.

CLARE. You harm me and there'll be criminal assault charges added to my court complaint.

VIOLET. Let her go, Myrah.

MYRAH. Sure. Just as soon as she makes a few promises.

CLARE. Like what?

MYRAH. Like leaving. Now! Immediately!

(**WINIFRED** *opens the washroom door, peers out*)

CLARE. Winifred!

WINIFRED. *(screaming hysterically)* Clare! Her head's floating– with only half a body!

(gives piercing scream and crumples behind doors)

VIOLET. Oh dear, I think she's fainted again.

MYRAH. Take over, Violet, I'll go see what happened.

(**MYRAH** *goes to the washroom.*)

CLARE. Let me out so I can help Winifred.

VIOLET. Myrah said–

CLARE. I just want to see her. I haven't seen her in over a year.

VIOLET. And, you won't take her away. Promise.

CLARE. Anything! Just let me out of here!

VIOLET. And you won't show her the telegram?

CLARE. I'll give you the telegram.

VIOLET. Right now?

CLARE. Yes. Just open this window, so I can get it out of my jacket pocket.

VIOLET. I don't know–

CLARE. I can't breathe. Do you want me to die!

VIOLET. Of course not.

CLARE. I have heart problems!

VIOLET. Well, all right. But you must promise to go away, leave Winifred alone.

CLARE. Anything. Hurry!

VIOLET. *(pulls lock tabs)* Oh dear, I think Myrah's returning.

> *(**CLARE** hurriedly pulls out of window and disappears.
> **VIOLET** is turned away.)*

MYRAH. What the!! Where'd she go?

VIOLET. *(innocently)* Who?

MYRAH. You know damn well who!

> *(**MYRAH** goes to window, opens it, looks out)*

Down that fire escape already, like a greased monkey.

VIOLET. She said she had heart trouble.

MYRAH. Yeah, hardening of the heart. We coulda made her promise anything.

VIOLET. She did. I made her promise–

MYRAH. Now I got no other plan, 'cept hoping she leaves by four.

> *(**WINIFRED** wanders out of the washroom. She's taken off
> **VIOLET**'s coat, now wearing just a camisole slip. There's
> an air of a child about her, as if they were strangers.)*

WINIFRED. Hello–

VIOLET. Winifred–

MYRAH. Felling better now?

WINIFRED. *(brightly and airily, with childish delight)* Look! Look at all the sunbeams!

> *(whirls about)*

The whole room– filled with beautiful dancing sunbeams.

MYRAH. Maybe I should try some of her medicine.

WINIFRED. *(running about, trying to capture sunbeams in her hand)* I caught one! There's another! Who wants to play with me? We'll catch all the sunbeams and put them into mama's crystal jar, turning into twinkling fireflies, sparkling in the moonlight. *(giggles airily)*

VIOLET. *(not sure what to make of it all)* How– interesting.

WINIFRED. It really happens. Come on, help me. Before they fly home to Mother Sun.

VIOLET. *(grabs for some)* I caught one.

MYRAH. They're gonna bust the door down– take us to jail– and you two are running around catching sunbeams.

*(As **VIOLET** is reaching for sunbeams, she stumbles over the dress box near the bottom of the furniture pile, falls to the floor, wedding dress spills out.)*

VIOLET. Oh dear, I missed one.

WINIFRED. *(rushes over)* Look! All the sunbeams landed in a beautiful golden pile.

VIOLET. Excuse me. I'm going to sit the rest of this game out. *(sits, rubbing wrist)*

WINIFRED. –And turned themselves into a lovely gown of golden sunshine. *(holds dress to her)*

MYRAH. *(shakes head slowly)* Never seen things like other people, did you Winifred.

WINIFRED. Can I try it on? Please?

MYRAH. Sure. Go ahead.

WINIFRED. Don't go away. I'll surprise you in a little bit. **(WINIFRED** *takes dress and bag and goes into washroom)*

MYRAH. Few more surprises– just what I need.

VIOLET. Poor child.

MYRAH. Never been this bad.

VIOLET. She really should be home. She needs to rest– or something.

MYRAH. Just hang on– Bunny Two Shoes gotta go feed those hungry hounds –

VIOLET. I mean it, Myrah, I'll take Winifred down that fire escape myself, if I have to.

MYRAH. You'd never make it. Don't know how Clare and all her blubber did, 'cept maybe her hands got claws.

VIOLET. We can't just sit here and do nothing.

MYRAH. Geez, I never seen you all riled like this before.

VIOLET. *(fast and rising in pitch)* My doll has been broken. Our friend Winifred is being threatened. My last dividend check was stolen right from my mailbox. They're going to shut off my electricity. Tax people are trying to take my house away from me.

(**VIOLET** *gives dress box a vicious kick*)

Is it any wonder my insides are churning!

MYRAH. Here, let me buy you a cup of coffee, something for your nerves.

VIOLET. Mama never got upset.

MYRAH. Hey, come on over and help. Gotta move this lounge to get at the coffee machine.

VIOLET. All right.

(**VIOLET** *attempts to help, but pain is too great*)

I can't. My wrist– I hurt it, when I fell.

MYRAH. My god, girl! All swelled up. You sprained it– or even broke it. Don't it hurt?

VIOLET. A little.

MYRAH. Hafta try myself then. *(tries shoving lounge)* Damn thing's like a ton of lead. Me with this rotten arthritis. No way I can do it alone.

(**MYRAH** *pounds fist on lounge in anger*)

VIOLET. Careful, Myrah.

MYRAH. What for? Criminy! Know what we did? Blockaded *ourselves* in here. (*laughs and half cries*) How the hell do we sneak out now!

VIOLET. We're going to need help– soon. My wrist is throbbing.

MYRAH. Who? Who we gonna get to help?

VIOLET. All we need is one strong person.

MYRAH. Yeah– who might that be?

VIOLET. Clare's very strong.

MYRAH. *(shrieks of laughter)* Clare! How the hell's she gonna help us get out, when she's trying to get in herself.

VIOLET. She can come up the fire escape, like before.

MYRAH. What's the matter with you, Violet, asking the enemy for help. You don't win wars that way.

VIOLET. I don't care about winning. I just want to go home. And so does Winifred.

CLARE. *(pounding on door)* All right, ladies. One last chance before we begin the drilling.

VIOLET. Go on, ask her.

(sounds of drill around door lock)

MYRAH. Drill all you want, you still won't get through.

VIOLET. My wrist, Myrah.

MYRAH. Stop your whimpering, Violet. Can't stand people what whimper.

*(**VIOLET** stands up and starts screaming. Every anguish in her life pouring out.)*

VIOLET. Aaaaaaaaah! Is that better? Better than whimpering.

MYRAH. Will you just–

*(unintentionally grabs Violet's sore wrist, **VIOLET** cries out in agony)*

I'm sorry, Violet. I didn't mean to hurt you. I never want to hurt nobody.

VIOLET. That is not true. You hurt people's feelings all the time, then laugh it off– just like your father!

MYRAH. I am not like my father! *(pauses in moment of realization)* Oh, all right. *(shouting with frustrated anger)* Can you– can you get back in here? Violet's hurt.

CLARE. *(drilling stops)* Just open this door if you want me in there.

MYRAH. Can't. All blocked up. We need help moving the stuff.

VIOLET. Come in through the window again. Winifred needs to get home.

CLARE. This better not be another one of your tricks. *(voice trails off)*

MYRAH. You satisfied now! Make you happy we're letting the enemy in! *(opens window wider)* Be her show from now on.

(sits, dfeated for first time)

Well, might as well get ready to go to jail. Just hope

I can get somebody to take care of Rags. *(noting* **VIO-LET***'s wrist)* Here, let's tie up that swelling.

VIOLET. It was the only possible solution.

MYRAH. You didn't even give me a chance to– Well, done is done. Past is past.

*(***MYRAH*** looks about for something to use, takes off pettipants.)*

Hell, might as well put em out where people can see em.

*(***MYRAH*** bandages Violet's wrist with pettipants.)*

VIOLET. Myrah, don't worry, you won't have to go to jail.

MYRAH. Tell that to the judge.

VIOLET. You won't have to go– because I will.

MYRAH. What?

VIOLET. If there are any charges, I'll confess. Tell them I kept you both here, against your wills.

MYRAH. What the hell you talking about?

VIOLET. I said, I would go to jail.

MYRAH. Lost all your screws. You never been near one of those stink holes.

VIOLET. You said they even had television. It can't be that bad.

MYRAH. Jail ain't no place for a lady like you.

VIOLET. I'm strong, Myrah. I just found that out today.

MYRAH. Ain't nobody strong enough for those cesspools.

VIOLET. I've already made up my mind.

MYRAH. *(her old spirit back, a challenge again)* You listen to me, Violet, anybody goes to jail, it's going to be *me*!

VIOLET. But– you said you couldn't take it anymore.

MYRAH. How do you think I'd feel, trying to have a good time, knowing you were rotting away in some rat-hole jail. You're not tough enough for those places, Violet. *(old verve back)* But, by god, I still am!!

(raises **VIOLET***'s pettipants-wrapped arm.)*

Semper Fi Delis!

CLARE. *(coming through window)* All right, where is she?

(Singing is heard. **WINIFRED** *enters. She looks radiant. Her hair is combed and softly held back with a yellow ribbon. Her dress is dried and billowing.)*

WINIFRED. *(singing brightly as a child)*

"Twinkle, twinkle, little star–

How I wonder what you are– Up above–

(**WINIFRED** *notices them, a moment of puzzlement)*

The world– so high– "

(stops)

CLARE. *(not sure what to do)* Winifred–

WINIFRED. *(to all three, light airy voice)* Did you come for the wedding?

MYRAH. What wedding?

WINIFRED. Mine. Today's May first.

VIOLET. Oh. You're a lovely looking bride.

WINIFRED. Where's Henry? Has he arrived yet?

VIOLET. Not yet dear.

WINIFRED. He was going to bring the daffodils.

MYRAH. *(clearing her throat)* Violet, why don't you take the bride in there– fix her veil and stuff. While Clare and I move away this furniture– so the guests can get through.

VIOLET. Come along. We'll find something old, and something new.

*(**VIOLET** and **WINIFRED** go into the washroom.)*

CLARE. See what you've done to her! Made her regress– all the way back to her wedding day.

MYRAH. So what! If it was a happy day, what's wrong with living it all over again?

CLARE. You are so ignorant about–

MYRAH. *(interrupting)* Let's get the furniture moving, okay!

CLARE. Then what happens?

MYRAH. Then you go back to your kennels, without Winifred.

CLARE. *(stops still)* No! Winifred's going with me!

MYRAH. But, you said–

CLARE. I said nothing. Anyone can see Winifred's not capable of caring for herself.

MYRAH. Sure. Anyone can see, but *you're* not going to. (**MYRAH** *quickly grabs Clare's glasses off her face.*)

CLARE. My glasses!

MYRAH. You'll get them back. But not till you're in that van– without Winifred.

CLARE. I came back here to help you, and–

MYRAH. So start helping then. We'll begin with the lounge.

CLARE. *(stubbornly stands still, arms crossed)* I am not moving one thing!

MYRAH. Don't want to help, huh! Lets's see if smashing your specs might change your mind. One– two–

CLARE. Wait! I need them to drive!

MYRAH. *(puts glasses down bosom of dress, grabs leash around Clare's waist)* Okay, let's get the furniture moving then. We move this to the right.

(they begin moving furniture)

CLARE. You're going to regret this.

MYRAH. Not one single minute of it.

CLARE. Well, I regret Winifred ever met up with you two.

MYRAH. Cut the yapping and come along, like a nice little doggie. And, after this furniture's moved, you go tell the store officials–

CLARE. I never told. They were all at some celebration.

MYRAH. Then, nobody at Rosenblooms knows?

CLARE. I got the drill from the janitor's closet myself.

MYRAH. Boy, I knew this was my lucky day!

(**VIOLET** *comes out of the washroom.*)

VIOLET. Winifred– she's not a bride anymore.

(**WINIFRED** *enters, new weariness about her*)

WINIFRED. I think it's time I went home. *(noticing **CLARE**, back into focus)* Clare–

MYRAH. Had to let her in, to help you get out.

VIOLET. But, she's not taking you away.

WINIFRED. I've never seen you without your glasses.

CLARE. She took them.

WINIFRED. Your eyes– they're not so frightening anymore.

CLARE. *(her threatening tone)* Winifred!

WINIFRED. In fact, you don't frighten me at all. I don't know why, but I feel– just so very different.

VIOLET. And you look lovely.

MYRAH. Sit down and relax, Winifred. We'll get this furniture out of the way real quick. Then Violet and I are gonna take you home.

WINIFRED. *(a new sense of surety, sits down)* It's all right. I'll go with Clare. There's no need to wait for Henry anymore. *(with resigned finality)* He's never coming back....

VIOLET. Who told you that?

WINIFRED. Nobody. Today was the day. There was supposesd to be a sign. A special sign, from Henry.

MYRAH. Day's not over yet.

VIOLET. You can't give up now, Winifred. Not after all these years.

MYRAH. Can't just up and leave your house. Why– your birds need you.

VIOLET. *(trying to cheer her up)* Teensy little bird out there right now. You certainly seem to attract them.

WINIFRED. *(shaken from her reality, comes to window)* A bird? Where?

VIOLET. Right there. Drinking up the rain water.

WINIFRED. *(exalted)* Why, it's a blue bird!

VIOLET. *(puzzled)* A blue bird?

MYRAH. Looks kinda like a sparrow to me.

WINIFRED. *(smiling radiantly)* My sign! From Henry!

VIOLET. Henry?

WINIFRED. Yes. I was his little canary. He was my blue bird–
My Blue Bird of Happiness.

MYRAH. Oh.

WINIFRED. We both saw one, the day we were married, in
Honeysuckle Park. I've never seen one since.

VIOLET. Strange– water reflecting on his wet feathers, does
make him appear blue.

MYRAH. Sure. He could be blue. Anybody can see he could
be a blue sparrow.

CLARE. Give me my glasses, so I can see the blue bird too.

MYRAH. Uh uh. You ain't wrecking this dream for her.

WINIFRED. *(still exalted)* Let Clare see the blue bird. She's
never ever seen one.

MYRAH. *(reluctantly)* Okay. if you want her to.

> (**MYRAH** *guides* **CLARE** *to window, holds glasses far in
> front of her eyes)*

See the birdie!

CLARE. *(scoffing)* Why, it's only a–

> *(stops, looks at* **MYRAH** *who's threatening to break her
> glasses)*

–A blue bird. That's what it is– a blue bird.

WINIFRED. From Henry.

CLARE. Yes, from Henry.

MYRAH. Well, we gonna stand round here all day, looking
at birds? Furniture to be moved.

> *(All of a sudden, band music strikes up in the distance,
> a rousing concert tune with lots of drums.)*

WINIFRED. I hear war music again–

VIOLET. *(at window)* The celebration, it's beginning already,
in Arcadia Park. They even have television cameras.
Spotlights.

WINIFRED. *(to window)* I see soldiers. One of them might
be Henry!

> (**WINIFRED** *starts climbing out the window.)*

VIOLET. Oh dear, she's going out the window again.

MYRAH. Winifred, get back in here!

CLARE. Go after her!

WINIFRED. *(calling from balcony, plaintively)* Henry– Henry! Here I am.

CLARE. Well, I'm not going to just stand by and watch

.   *(CLARE starts climbing out the window)*

   Somebody! Help! My sister's going to jumps from this balcony!

MYRAH. Let's get rid of you once and for all!

   (MYRAH grabs CLARE by her by leash. She throws her fur jacket over her head, yanking her by the sleeves and forcefully pushes her into washroom. She shuts and bolts door. Clare's shouting and pounding is muffled.)

MYRAH. Now, let's take care of Winifred.

   (Bright circling lights begin circling the window area. A bullhorn calls from below.)

VOICES. Don't jump lady! Don't jump!

VIOLET. TV cameras, they're aimed up here now. Winifred, she's just standing there, stiff as a statue.

MYRAH. Get me that birdcage.

   (MYRAH takes cage and stands at window)

   Winifred– Romeo's calling you.

VOICES BELOW. "What's going on up there?"

   "Some old lady's going to jump!"

   "There's another one– with a birdcage!"

TV VOICE. Can you hear me up there?

MYRAH. Yeah, we can hear you, and you're all gonna hear from me in one cotton-picking minute. Come on Winifred, back inside.

   (MYRAH leads WINIFRED back in. Noise below continues.)

   Violet, take over!

TV VOICE. Attention! This is WKOT-TV. Could you tell our viewers why that woman was going to jump. What did you do to stop her? Cameras are on you! Go!

(Clapping and cheering, which continues.)

MYRAH. *(out on ledge, using cane for emphasis)* My name is Myrah Gordon. And I'm speaking for all my friends. Winifred, and Violet, and Angie, what works at the bus depot, and Hattie, who lives next door to me and can't get out of her room. And Minnie the Bag Lady– and all the other old–

TV VOICE. All we want to know is– Why was the lady going to jump?

MYRAH. You wanta know why an old lady would wanta jump from a department store balcony? Lots of reasons– if you're old and live in America–

(band music starts again)

TV VOICE. Thank you very much! Myrah Gordon– from Rosenblooms rest room. Now, back to our celebration.

(Lights are gone and the cheering fades.)

MYRAH. Cut me off, you s.o.b. I don't need your TV cameras!

(steps back into rest room, but it's as if she's still addressing the crowds outside)

I'm gonna make my voice heard clear across this country! Whatever it takes. 'Cause once you reach sixty– get a few gray hairs, coupla wrinkles, you ain't no good anymore.

(lifts cane as flag staff)

But that's okay, because we're tough! We can take it, if we made it this far. So, stop bossing us around!

(pounds cane emphatically)

Some day, you're all gonna be our age too. No way you can stop it! So we're gonna keep fighting, for ourselves, and for you. Keep this the land of the free– the home of the brave! Semper Fidelis!!!

(raises cane in one grand swirl, smiles as if bowing to her audience)

God bless America!

VIOLET. You really said it all, Myrah.

MYRAH. Aagh, let's get outa here. Once that speech hits the TV–

VIOLET. Once it does, I'm sure they won't let us back in here anymore.

MYRAH. So what! Let them keep their fancy-dancy rest room. Turn it into a video parlor– Who cares!

VIOLET. You're right. Who cares!

MYRAH. Hell, I been thinking, there's that Goldman's Department Store, down the street. Rest room ain't as big, but heck, was getting sick of looking at these same four walls day after day.

WINIFRED. I think I've had enough celebrating.

MYRAH. Haven't we all.

WINIFRED. I think I'll go to the zoo another day.

VIOLET. Of course, dear. There's always another day.

(**MYRAH** *takes last chair away from the door and swings it open.*)

MYRAH. Okay, you two, get going!

(*music starts up again, "There'll Be A Hot Time in The Old Town Tonight*)

(**VIOLET** *gathers her things.* **WINIFRED** *stands with bird cage.*)

MYRAH. Hey, Violet, why don't you take Winifred on over to Arcadia Park. Sit for awhile. I'll join you in a jiffy.

(**MYRAH** *pulls out a twenty dollar bill and Clare's glasses from bosom, waves bill*)

Then, if we got any pep left, we're gonna take Winifred to "Wild Bill's Bar and Grill." Give her a real anniversary celebration.

(**MYRAH** *gives* **WINIFRED** *and* **VIOLET** *both a big hug*)

Now, take your doll and bird and get the hell outa here!

(**MYRAH** *watches them leave, then swings into action.*)

(*following is done very swiftly.* **MYRAH** *gathers Winifred's leftover things, her own shopping bag, cane, puts on her hat, looks around*)

MYRAH. Rats! My fur! *(starts to go to the washroom)* Aagh, let her and the dogs have that moth-eaten old thing.

(*stops and places Clare's glasses on the coffee table, with Clare's umbrella, shouting to washroom*)

Okay, Clare de Lune– the rest roo m is yours! *(final sweeping wave)* So long Rosenblooms! It's been good to know ya!

"Done is done, past is past–

Future's only thing that lasts!"

(*unbolts washroom door, then runs like hell, with bag and cane through EXIT door, as washroom door is forcefully pushed open by* **CLARE**. *Store SOUNDS are heard, loud bang of other door closing*)

(*QUICK CURTAIN!*)

The End

COSTUME AND PERSONAL PROPERTY LIST

MYRAH

Wears ratty fur jacket
    Cheap silky print dress
    Lots of flashy jewelry
    Black frayed slip shows
    Under slip is red pettipants
    Stockings have runs
    High heeled shoes, turned over at edges
    Floppy springlike hat covering yellowed blonde hair and drooping hairset
    Heavy makeup masks once-pretty features

Carries bulging shopping bag and wooden cane
 Inside bag
    Plastic bag with grapes
    Aerosol spray can
    Super market tabloid paper
    Tribune newspaper
    Eyebrow pencil
    Large hymn book
    Lotto game
    Long colorful silky Tango scarf

VIOLET

Wears dated purple velvet coat
    Sprig of violets pinned to lapel
    Lacy lavender blouse
    Purple skirt
    Light colored sandals
    Lavender gloves, purse
    Amethyst jewelry

Carries
    Purple umbrella
    Several homemade bags of worn brocade
 Inside bags
    Bouquet of lilacs
    Small jar for lilacs
    Embroidery items
    Vigil candle and matches
    Picnic items
    Handkerchief
Old suitcase-like box
 Inside box
    Beautiful French doll dressed in lavender

(Any modern doll, dressed in long lacy dress and wide brimmed lacy bonnet will give an "antique appearance.")

WINIFRED
Wears billowing summer dress in faded yellow voile
(More practical to have a two piece dress. Billowing skirt and long sleeved blouse, so there's a dry skirt to exchange for wet one.)
Flowing gold cape that resembles huge bird wings when arms are raised
Camisole slip under dress
Bright yellow ribbon holds back gold/gray hair, styled in an uneven page-boy hairdo

Carries
Old fashioned birdcage. Two canaries inside
Gold carry bag
Inside bag
Assorted loose mail
Binoculars
Medicine bottle
Old letters tied with yellow ribbon

CLARE
Wears brown uniform type outfit
"Clare's Canine Campus" embroidered across back of jacket
Thick-lensed glasses
Silver whistle on heavy cord around her neck
Trailing dog leash around her waist
White fur shoes

Carries
Large black umbrella
Telegram in pocket (yellow)

PATRON (All in Act I)
1 – Shopping clothes. Carries bright flowery bag with "ROSEN-BLOOMS" in large letters

2 – Minnie the Moocher. Old lady in weatherbeaten clothes
Mismatched, oversized shoes
Ankle socks
Ragged black coat
Scraggly hair
Clutching grungy shopping bag
3 – Regular dress. Tired look
4 – Mod outfit. Short skirt, boots, sunglasses
5 – Regular dress
6 – Brown coat, white shoes
Carries boom box and wears huge red earphones
7 – Elegantly dressed

8 – Regular dress
9 – Regular dress.
    Purse with $20 bill

PROPERTY PLOT

ONSTAGE:

FURNITURE
Candy machine with mirror
    (Need not be real or working. But should be rigged so Lifesavers fall
    out when piece of cardboard or other device is removed. Same for
    coins. Someone could also feed items from behind.)
Coffee machine or Mr. Coffee
Drinking fountain
Window that opens
    (Important to have lightweight frame. No glass. Strips of foam rubber
    on top and bottom of sill, to protect Clare when captured.)
Coffee table (center), with dish and magazines atop
Three chairs around coffee table
Arm chair to side
Lounge or settee
Desk and chair
Large plant, small potted plants
Manikins
Large pillow
Various floor lamps

OFFSTAGE PROPS
Metal scrub pail
Paper cups
Huge dress box
"OUT OF ORDER" sign

From the Reviews of
IN THE REST ROOM
AT ROSENBLOOMS...

"The women are wonderful characters...[the play does]
an excellent job of balancing humor against the basically
pathetic lives of the three main characters."
- Minneapolis Tribune

"A very funny play of character and situations. You can't
get much better than that writingwise: check out William
Shakespeare..."
- Appleton Post Crescent

"Visit to *Rosenblooms* is worth the trip. Quirky characters,
punchy lines and light hearted humor."
- Driftwood News, Canada

"Hilarious one minute and surpisingly touching the next."
- Gallery Theatre, California

"Maybe the best comedy is the one that makes you cry. This
Ludmilla Bollow script is an almost perfect example of the
classic dramatic unities of time and place."
- Neenah Post Crescent

"It's comedy, but has very poignant moments in it as well."
- Go-Erie.com

Winner of the Southeastern Theatre Conference
New Play Award